Praise for Christmas

Praise Him Anyhow Series

Praise for Christmas

Vanessa Miller

Book 6
Praise Him Anyhow Series

Other Books by Vanessa Miller

After the Rain
How Sweet The Sound
Heirs of Rebellion
Feels Like Heaven
Heaven on Earth
The Best of All
Better for Us
Her Good Thing
Long Time Coming
A Promise of Forever Love
A Love for Tomorrow
Yesterday's Promise
Forgotten
Forgiven
Forsaken
Rain for Christmas (Novella)
Through the Storm
Rain Storm
Latter Rain
Abundant Rain
Former Rain

Anthologies (Editor)
Keeping the Faith
Have A Little Faith
This Far by Faith

EBOOKS

Love Isn't Enough

A Mighty Love

The Blessed One (Blessed and Highly Favored series)

The Wild One (Blessed and Highly Favored Series)

The Preacher's Choice (Blessed and Highly Favored Series)

The Politician's Wife (Blessed and Highly Favored Series)

The Playboy's Redemption (Blessed and Highly Favored Series)

Tears Fall at Night (Praise Him Anyhow Series)

Joy Comes in the Morning (Praise Him Anyhow Series)

A Forever Kind of Love (Praise Him Anyhow Series)

Ramsey's Praise (Praise Him Anyhow Series)

Escape to Love (Praise Him Anyhow Series)

Praise For Christmas (Praise Him Anyhow Series)

His Love Walk (Praise Him Anyhow Series)

Could This Be Love (Praise Him Anyhow Series)

Song of Praise (Praise Him Anyhow Series)

Chapter 1

Carmella Marshall-Thomas, leaned over to take a French vanilla cake out of the oven. The counter was now lined with three cakes for her step-daughter, Renee Thomas, soon to be Renee Morris, to sample.

"Couldn't I just have three different layers?" Renee asked with the fork in her hand. She had just sampled the chocolate fudge and the strawberry cake. "Those two are delicious and I know I'm going to love this French vanilla also."

Taking the oven mitts off her hands, Carmella flexed her fingers and then began rubbing her hands. "Well, you need to make a decision fast; your wedding is only three weeks away."

"Tell me about it. I can hardly believe that Thanksgiving was last week. Everything is moving so fast." Renee was about to sample the French vanilla, but as she glanced up at Carmella, she put her fork down and asked, "Are you okay? Why do you keep rubbing your hands like that?"

Carmella looked down at her hands. She hadn't realized that she was rubbing her hands. She began flexing them as she answered, "I'm trying to get some circulation going in them. They've been numbing up on me from time to time and a baker needs her hands."

"I know that's right. Those hands better not go numbing-up while you're fixing my wedding cake."

"Don't worry. I'll make sure this wedding cake is absolute perfection. I just have to face the fact that I'm getting older." She lifted the eyeglasses that were hanging around her neck. "I've even started using reading glasses."

"I didn't know you were having problems with your vision."

"Every now and then things look a little blurry. But these reading glasses work wonders."

"Have you had your eyes checked recently?" Renee asked as she bit into the French vanilla cake.

"I haven't gone to the eye doctor, but I just had my annual physical." Carmella waved away thoughts of one more appointment in the middle of all that she had to do in the next few weeks. "I'm fine. Can't expect to have the same twenty-twenty vision in my fifties like I had in my thirties."

"Oh my goodness, Mama Carmella this French vanilla cake is the bomb.com, as Tamar Braxton would say."

"So it sounds like you've made a decision."

"Well I think French vanilla is the winner, but I'm going to take a piece of each cake to Jay to see if he agrees with me."

"Smart girl. I love the fact that you are thinking about Jay during this process. Because if you remember nothing else I tell you, please remember this... a beautiful wedding means nothing if the marriage is a disaster."

"I'm taking my cues from you and Dad."

Carmella and Renee were in the kitchen/prep area for Hallelujah Cakes and Such. Carmella's bakery had become a huge hit in the shopping center not far from her home. It was such a hit that Carmella and her husband, Ramsey were working on a business plan to expand the business to two or three other locations. God had been so good to her, that Carmella couldn't possibly tell it all if she tried.

"Let's discuss the rehearsal dinner. What kind of food do you want me to serve?" The phone rang. Carmella started working on the frosting for Renee's cake confident that Mary, her front of the store manager would answer the phone.

"Thanksgiving dinner was so delicious, and I was thinking that since everyone is going to be doing their own thing for Christmas, why don't we do it the rehearsal dinner like one of your Christmas dinners."

It saddened Carmella to think about Christmas this year. Since Dontae and Jewel had been with them for Thanksgiving, they were going to be with Jewel's family for Christmas. The same was true for Ramsey and Maxine. Renee would be on her honeymoon. Ronnie was acting like he was the President of the United States, with so many responsibilities that he didn't spend Thanksgiving with his family, nor was he planning to come home for Christmas. Rashawn was still on the mission field, but Carmella was still holding out hope that he would be able to come home this year. "You're right about that. Seems like it will only be Joy, Lance and Raven coming to the house for Christmas dinner this year."

"So why not do it up at the rehearsal dinner?"

"Yeah, why not. We'll do a turkey, dressing, candied yams... the works."

"And don't forget about the cheese rolls you make."

Mary poked her head in the kitchen. "The phone's for you, Carmella."

Carmella handed the mixer to Renee and pointed at the bowl she'd started her cream cheese frosting in. "Getting to mixing, girl."

Renee grabbed the mixer and went to work on the frosting. Tamela Mann's *I Can Only Imagine* song came on the radio and Renee hummed while she worked.

Carmella put the phone to her ear and said, "This is Carmella Thomas, may I help you?"

"Hi, Mrs. Thomas, this is Sabrina, how are you doing?"

The only Sabrina Carmella knew was the nurse at her doctor's office. She had been going to the same doctor for the past ten years. Carmella had never missed an annual exam, but she had also never received a call after one of those exams either. They always just mailed the results to her, so now she wondered what this call was all about. "Hey Sabrina, I'm doing good. What's going on?"

"I'm just calling because Dr. Mika would like to see you so she can go over your test results."

"Why don't you just mail them to me? We have so much going on now, that I don't want to fit another thing in my schedule."

"The thing is," Sabrina began, "Dr. Mika really wants to sit down and talk to you about some of the results."

Carmella's heart felt as if it dropped to her feet. Something was wrong. Something was *very* wrong. *God Will Make A Way,* by Shirley Caesar started playing as Carmella closed her eyes and silently prayed, Lord Jesus, I sure need you right now. See me through whatever this is.

***

"Wake up, Dontae, it's time," Jewel said as she shoved her husband.

Dontae Marshall sat up in bed, rubbed his eyes and then turned to Jewel. "Time for what?"

"The baby, silly. I've been having contractions all night."

Shaking his head, Dontae told her, "It's not time. You're not due until next week."

"Tell your son or daughter that. Because these contractions are kicking my butt." As she said that another contraction started. Jewel started breathing hard. She grabbed hold of Dontae's hand and squeezed the life out of it.

Dontae pulled his hand away from her and jumped out of bed. "Oh my God, this is really happening." He started aimlessly roaming around the room, mumbling to himself.

"Um, baby, I'm going to need you to stick with the plan. This is no time for you to freak out, okay?"

What was she talking about? As far as Dontae was concerned, this was the perfect time to freak out. His wife was having their first child and he had no clue how to be a father. Would he be a good one like Ramsey had been to his five kids, or would he lose his mind after a few years and go AWOL like his father had done when he left his mother years ago?

"Awww!" Jewel yelled as she gripped her stomach.

Dontae grabbed his stomach and doubled over as if he had just been gut punched by a three-hundred pound linebacker.

Rolling her eyes heavenward, Jewel picked up the phone and dialed her sister, Maxine. Jewel's other sister, Dawn was out of town and even though Maxine had her hands full with Brielle, she said she would help when the time came. It was five in the morning, but Maxine had promised to answer at any time of the night or day.

"Is it time?" a groggy Maxine asked as she answered the phone.

"Yes, and my husband is over here acting as if he's the one that has gone into labor."

"I'm sorry, Jewel," Dontae said, still holding his stomach. "But an awful pain just went through me. Just give me a minute and I'll get it together."

Jewel shook her head as Maxine said, "Didn't I tell you he was going to act like this? He's such a drama king."

Jewel laughed. "I need you, Maxie. Can you meet us at the hospital?"

"Are you sure you don't need me to come over there and drive you to the hospital? If Dontae is flipping out, he might not be able to drive the car."

"Unless he wants to deliver this baby in our bedroom, he'd better get it together and get me to the hospital."

"I got this. I got this." Dontae rushed over to the bed and helped Jewel up. "Do you need me to help you put on some clothes?"

"I'm wearing this gown, just give me my coat."

Dontae wanted to protest Jewel leaving the house in her nightgown, but the look on her face told him that this was not the right time to mess with her. So he simply said, "Yes, dear." As they headed out of the house, Dontae realized that this was the day that he would finally become a man in every sense of the word... was he ready for that?

Chapter 2

Lance Bryant hung up the phone and waited for his wife to get out of the shower. He paced back and forth in front of the bathroom door, hoping that she would hurry so he wouldn't have to rush into the bathroom and tell her his news. He would look too eager if he did that... needed to play it cool.

He heard the shower water turn off, clenched his hands in anticipation, then went into their walk-in closet, pretending as if he was really looking for something in there, grabbed a pair of brown socks and then headed back into the bedroom as he heard the bathroom door open. He sat down on the bed and began putting on his socks as Joy rummaged through the dresser drawer. "I've got good news for you," Lance said.

"What's up?" She pulled a mauve tank top out of the drawer and slid it over her head.

"Dontae called. Jewel just had the baby." He couldn't keep the excitement out of his voice as he said, "It's a girl!"

"That's great. I'll send them a gift for the baby." Joy's voice didn't hold the same enthusiasm as her husband's. She slipped into her skirt and was about to put on her jacket when...

"I thought we'd take the day off and drive down to Charlotte to see our baby niece."

"No," was all Joy said before walking out of their bedroom and heading to the kitchen.

Lance was on her heels. "What do you mean, 'no'? Your brother just had his first child. Aren't you excited about that?"

"Of course I'm excited. But I have a full schedule. I just can't drop everything and go on a play date with my baby brother and his family. You have a lot on your plate this week also. So, I really don't see how your suggestion will benefit us."

"Why does everything have to benefit us? Why can't we just do something, anything in life just because we want to do it?" Lance threw up his hands and stormed back into the bedroom to finish dressing and put some distance between him and his wonderful wife.

Joy poured coffee into her mug, grabbed her keys and left the house as quickly as she could. Once she was a fair distance away from the house, Joy picked up her cell and called Dontae.

He answered on the first ring. "Lance told you our good news?"

"He sure did. I'm so happy for you and Jewel," she said and truly meant it. She had downplayed her happiness in the house with Lance, but now she could act as giddy as she wanted. "I can't believe that I have a niece. I'm not old enough to be anybody's auntie."

"Oh, you're old enough, all right. You're three years older than I am."

"Don't remind me. Time is getting away from me and I still have so much to accomplish. But enough about my age. What did you name the baby?"

"We named her Carmella Elizabeth. So, she has both her grandmother's names, but we will most likely call her Cammie."

Tears instantly sprang to Joy's eyes. "I bet Mama was so happy when you told her about little Cammie."

"She started crying."

"I bet she did. I'm crying myself. Matter-of-fact, I need to pull this car over before I run into someone." Once she pulled over, she said, "I wish I could be there but I can't leave work right now."

"Don't worry about it, sis. We will be in Raleigh in two weeks for Renee's wedding."

"Can you do me a favor and text me a picture of her?"

"Okay, I'll do it now. So, check your phone in about a minute."

Joy couldn't make herself pull her car back into traffic. She waited, counting down the seconds until the ding on her phone alerted her to the fact that she had a text. She opened the text, clicked on the picture and smiled even as the tears flowed again, while she lovingly gazed at the picture of her beautiful niece.

***

Carmella and Ramsey sat in her doctor's office, holding hands and waiting for her doctor to come into the room.

"Your hands are shaking, Carmella. Stop that. Everything is going to be just fine. You wait and see," Ramsey tried to reassure her.

"I know. I guess I'm just nervous. I've never been called back to the doctor's office after an annual checkup before."

"Well, before we jump to any wrong conclusions, let's just hear what the doctor has to say."

Ramsey was right, she was worrying herself for nothing, when what she needed to be doing was making plans to go see her namesake. She and Ramsey were already grandparents due to Ram Jr.'s little girl, Brielle. But Brielle was over a year old before they were introduced to her. This would be the first grandchild that they would actually get to see as an infant... and she was named after her. Carmella was a proud grandma indeed. Her son had weathered his storms and now had a family who would love him for a lifetime.

The door opened and Dr. Mika walked in. She shook hands with Carmella and then Ramsey. "Nice to see you both."

"Pardon me for rushing the matter, Dr. Mika, but can you please tell me why I've been summoned back here?" Carmella wanted to get this over with, so she would know exactly what to put on her prayer list.

"I know how you are, Carmella. You don't want me to sugar coat things for you, so I'm going to lay it out. We did find a problem with your blood work."

Ramsey tightened his grip on Carmella's hands as she asked, "What kind of problem?"

"Your A1C is at 8.8."

"What's an A1C?" Ramsey wanted to know.

"Basically, I'm talking about your blood glucose levels. Normal levels are at about 5.6 or 5.7 at the highest. Levels at 6 to around 6.4 indicate pre-diabetes," Dr. Mika said.

"But my levels are higher than that. What does an 8.8 level indicate?" Carmella asked, knowing the answer before it was spoken into the atmosphere.

"You have diabetes."

Carmella blinked twice, trying her best not to cry, because she had just heard the words she had dreaded for a lifetime. Her mother had diabetes and died at sixty-two because of complications from it. "I don't understand. When I did my annual checkup last year, I wasn't even pre-diabetic. How did I skip that step?"

"I don't know how it happened, but we have to correct this problem immediately."

"What's your suggestion, Doc?" Ramsey asked.

Dr. Mika said, "I want to start you on medication... just a low dose for now so that we can regulate your blood sugar."

Too stunned to speak, Carmella looked around the office and then back to her doctor. She didn't know much about diabetes, but she knew her God. Shaking her head, she told Dr. Mika, "I don't want medication. I don't have diabetes."

"I'm sorry, Carmella but the test shows that you very clearly have this disease."

"I understand what your test says, but I'm thinking about my God and His ability to reverse any curse or disease that trying to attack my life."

Dr. Mika didn't say anything for a moment. Almost as if she didn't know what to say.

Carmella asked, "Do you have any recommendations for things I should do while I'm praying about this illness?"

"My suggestion would be medication, but I can't force you to take it." Dr. Mika tapped her pen against the table and then added, "Diet and exercise can help, but there's no cure for diabetes."

Carmella stood up and said, "I know too much about my God, Dr. Mika. I'm going to reverse this disease. Diabetes will not kill me."

Chapter 3

"Oh Ram, you should have seen her, she was so cute and precious," Maxine told Ramsey Jr, her husband of almost two years.

"I bet she was a cute little something." Ram laughed as he added, "Leave it to Dontae to suck up and name her after Mama Carmella."

Shoving his shoulder playfully, Maxine said, "Don't be jealous. I'm sure that Carmella and your father will love all of their grandchildren equally."

"They better." Ram pulled Maxine down into the oversized chair with him. "They already treat Brielle like a little princess. But they better not slack on the baby you and I are going to have just because Dontae is a suck up."

Maxine stiffened. She had wanted to have a serious talk with her husband but when he said things like that, she didn't know if her words would fall on deaf ears.

"I'm sorry, Maxine, I shouldn't have said that."

"It's okay. I know you didn't mean to upset me." She turned to him, eyes full of love, heart filled with trepidation. "I just think it's time for us to consider other options."

"No," Ramsey said as he stood up and gave his wife a determined look. "We just have to keep our faith in God. He knows our hearts' desire."

"All right, hon, we'll do it your way," Maxine said as she turned her head so that Ram couldn't see the tears in her eyes.

    ***

Carmella hadn't taken the medication that Dr. Mika recommended but she had picked up the blood glucose meter and strips that Dr. Mika suggested she use to check her levels three times a day. She had been given a little pamphlet to jot down her numbers. Since she didn't have any pharmaceutical medication, Carmella took a daily dose of the word of God as she meditated on healing scriptures every morning.

Today she was reading Jeremiah 17:14, *Heal me, O Lord, and I shall be healed; save me, and I shall be saved: for thou art my praise.*

Carmella had no doubt that the God she served was well able to save and heal her from this dreaded illness. Her mother had been diagnosed with diabetes when Carmella was in her early teens. She'd watched her mother take pills and then inject insulin into her body in hopes of curing the disease. But no medication had been invented to cure diabetes. So, instead of a cure, her mother eventually died from kidney complications related to her diabetes.

She had known people who had lost limbs and even gone blind because of this type of illness, and yet none of that knowledge had stopped her from adding ten extra pounds a year to her girth for the last five years. Her famous cakes, cookies and pies didn't just come out of her oven and go out to the masses. Carmella and Ramsey had eaten their fair share as well. But the difference between her and Ramsey was that he went to the gym and worked out regularly.

She laid her glucose meter on the bed, poked her finger with the devise that came with the meter. She then massaged her finger to extract enough blood to lay on the little strip. She placed the little blood bubble on the strip and then waited with expectancy for God to do His thing with the numbers.

She had been testing herself for the last three days each morning before she even put a morsel of food in her mouth, and each time the meter had read some crazy number that had been over two hundred. Carmella had gone on the internet and researched the types of foods she needed to eat in order to get the insulin levels in her body to line back up and act like they had some sense.

For years she'd heard diet gurus say that shoppers should stay on the outside aisles of the grocery store. Now she understood. Because all the foods that promised to reverse the curse of diabetes were in the vegetable and meat sections of the grocery store. The meter beeped and Carmella glanced down... 230.

Ramsey picked that moment to walk into the room. He glanced at her meter and said, "Are you sure you don't need the medication? I don't want to lose you, Carmella."

Putting her equipment back in the box she said, "You're not going to lose me. I plan to live a long time. We'll both be in here shuffling around on our walkers and seeing just how wonderful all of our grandchildren turned out."

"But your numbers haven't gone down. The doctor said that unchecked, diabetes could cause a heart attack or a stroke. Now faith is one thing, but using your God-given common sense to live is another."

Carmella loved Ramsey Thomas Sr. with everything that was in her. He was the man of her dreams. She thanked God every day for a man who loved her as much as Ramsey did. So, she wasn't going to condemn him just because his faith wasn't where hers was in this matter. After all, he was the one who would have to take care of her if she had a stroke. And he was the one who'd be left to grieve if she died from a heart attack. She softly touched his face and then leaned over and kissed him. When she pulled back from his warmth she asked, "Can we play let's make a deal?"

"What kind of deal?"

"Give me two weeks. I go back to see Dr. Mika on the twentieth. If I'm not better by that date, then I'll agree to take the medicine."

"The twentieth. That's the date of Renee's rehearsal dinner."

"Sure is. So, how about it? Do I have a deal? Will you let me do this my way?"

"For two weeks?"

"That's all I'm asking." Carmella smiled at him, hoping that he would take her smile as confidence.

"Okay, I'll give you two weeks, but those numbers better start going down or I just might change my mind."

She nodded while silently praying, *You heard him, Lord. We have to show Ramsey something, so help me out with my glucose numbers.* When Ramsey came out of their walk-in closet dressed in a jogging suit and gym shoes, she asked, "Are you getting ready to go workout?"

"Yep. Got to get my workout in before I begin my day."

He was so good with this stuff. "Can I work out with you today?"

Ramsey was tying his shoes; he turned to look at his wife. "Are you serious?"

"I'm serious, Ramsey. I am determined to get healthy. All the research I've found says that diabetes is mostly a lifestyle disease. So, I believe that we can turn my situation around by changing the foods that we eat and working out. So I'm going to need your help to keep me motivated on the workout tip."

Ramsey nodded. "That vegetable lasagna you fixed yesterday was banging, so I don't think I'll need much help with motivation when it comes to changing our diets. The way you cook, I'll eat anything you put in front of me."

"Thanks honey. Now let me make my smoothie and then I'll be ready to hit the gym with you."

"Are you putting those pomegranates and blueberries in your smoothie again?"

"I sure am, those two fruit are packed with antioxidants that my body needs to get my pancreas creating insulin like it's supposed to again, among other things."

"Sounds good. I think I'll take a protein shake this morning, also."

"Coming right up." Carmella jumped out of bed and headed to the kitchen with her mind set on changing circumstances. She wasn't going to be a cake-eating couch potato anymore. She took the steps like Rocky when as he trained for the fight of his life. Because that's just how she felt, but with God's help, Carmella planned to beat diabetes to death. She was going to tear the head off of her enemy and stop it in its tracks.

"Thank you, Jesus for reversing this curse. I am not diabetic and will not live in that state. You're an awesome God and to You and You alone goes all my praise."

***

"Thanks for seeing us, Dr. Reynolds. I don't know what I would have done if you had already left for your Christmas vacation," Renee said as she and Jay sat down on the couch.

"If you had called a day later I would have been gone to the cabin. We like to get away for about two weeks during this time of year. The wife likes for us to get in the Christmas spirit in a big way."

"Sounds nice," Jay said, "I've been so busy with the wedding and my company that I haven't even had the time to buy a tree."

"If I remember correctly, the two of you are going to be on an island, lying on the beach during Christmas. So, I wouldn't worry about getting a tree this year if I were you," Dr. Reynolds said.

"The tree isn't the problem," Renee told him. "It's the island. I'm afraid. I keep having nightmares." Renee had become a patient of Dr. Reynolds after the tragic events that occurred during her escape to the Bahamas last year. Her ex-boyfriend had followed her and tried to kill her and Jay. Most days Renee dealt with the trauma of the past by praying and putting it out of her mind. But ever since she and Jay decided to go back to the Bahamas, the place where they fell in love, Renee's nightmares had started up again. And therefore she felt compelled to see Dr. Reynolds one more time.

"Maybe I made a bad decision about our honeymoon trip," Jay said. "All I was thinking about was how beautiful the island is and how we finally admitted the feelings we had for each other over there."

Renee put a hand on Jay's face. "Your thought was sweet, and I love you all the more for it. This is something I need to conquer."

"I think you're right about this, Renee. Right now it sounds like you're dealing with fear. And God has not given us the spirit of fear, but what?"

Renee loved that her psychologist was a Christian. He always turned her back to the word of God. So, she happily finished the scripture he began for her... "but of power, and of love and of a sound mind."

Jay put his hand on Renee's shoulder as he said to Dr. Reynolds, "So what you're saying is, since this fear is not from God that Renee and I should go to the Bahamas?"

"No." Dr. Reynolds looked from Jay and then back to Renee. "The fear that you have is very real. Or at least the trauma that's causing the fear. You did shoot and kill your ex-boyfriend on that island."

She didn't like being reminded of the events that occurred on that island. But Renee knew one thing for sure, God had been with her. Because there is no way she would have survived if He hadn't been.

"So now you have to decide if you are willing to give that fear over to God. Because your ex-boyfriend can't hurt you anymore. But if you can't give it over to God, this might not be the time for the Bahamas," Dr. Reynolds added.

Leaning against Jay, Renee closed her eyes and took a deep breath. When she opened her eyes again,

Renee said, "Thank you, Dr. Reynolds, you've given me a lot to think and pray about."

Chapter 4

"I just don't know what I'm going to do, Mom. Lance has been in a mood ever since little Cammie was born," Joy said as she dunked her wheat donut in ice cold milk while she sat at a table with Carmella in Hallelujah Cakes and Such.

"Have you asked him what's wrong?"

"Don't need to. I already know what he's tripping on."

Carmella sipped her protein shake with pomegranates, blueberries, cinnamon and hemp seeds, all things that are good for regulating blood sugar levels.

"Look at me. I'm being a hog. I put three donuts on my plate and didn't even ask if you wanted one." Joy lifted her plate, offering Carmella one of the donuts.

"This is my breakfast." Carmella lifted the shake. "Protein and fruit does a body good."

"If you say so. I absolutely love your donuts and don't know what I would do without them," Joy said as she dunked and then took another bite out of her donut.

The funny thing was, Carmella would have said the same thing a month ago. She never would have thought that she could have gone off of sweets cold turkey, but once she stopped eating them, it was as if her body stopped craving them. She could work all day in her bakery, making the most deliciously sweet desserts and not even think about eating any of it. Carmella attributed that to God. He was giving her the grace she needed to get to the other side of this disease.

"What's Lance so upset about?" Carmella asked.

"He has been after me about having a baby and it's just gotten worse since Dontae had his baby."

"Joy, that's wonderful. I'd love to have another grandbaby. When are you going to start trying?"

"I'm not. That's why Lance has been so moody. He thinks I'm being selfish."

When handling her strong-willed daughter, Carmella tried very hard not to push. Joy would eventually make the right decision. Sometimes it just took her a little longer to see what right looked like. "Do *you* think you're being selfish?"

Joy shook her head. "Absolutely not. I'm being wise about the matter. All Lance can think about is having a house full of kids, but I'm busy building my career. I want to be a judge within the next ten years."

"I know you don't plan to wait ten years before having a child, Joy. Good Lord, you've already been married for seven years."

"You sound like Lance. All I hear from him is about how long we've been married without having kids. He doesn't even care that having kids will most likely hurt my career."

"Is that the only reason you don't want kids after seven years of marriage? Or is something else bothering you?"

Before Joy could answer, the door swung open and Renee bounced over to their table. "Hello ladies, I'm glad that both of you are here on time. We have tons to do and only a week left to do it."

"Then maybe next time you might try to be on time yourself," Joy responded.

"Whatever, I didn't complain during your wedding preparations when you bossed everyone around like we were your own personal servants. So, just smile sweetly and give me a hug even if I'm a few minutes late for the next few days. Okay, big sis?"

"You've got a deal. And I'm sorry for being a grouch. I was just taking my frustration out on you." Joy stood and hugged her sister.

"Okay, you two, let's get started, "Carmella said as her daughters sat down.

"Hey, where's my donuts?" Renee plucked a donut off of Joy's plate. "I love these things. Can you make some for the rehearsal dinner?"

"That's what I wanted to talk to you about," Carmella said, trying to tread lightly. She didn't want to do anything to make Renee's day feel any less special than Joy's had been. But she was learning so much, and feeling as if she was causing her family more harm than good. She wanted to start some new traditions and hoped that Renee would allow her to start at the rehearsal dinner. "I was thinking that we would go easy on the sweets and the pasta. I found this recipe for a spaghetti squash baked with cheese. It tastes a lot like the au gratin potatoes that I used to make."

"What do you mean, used to make. I thought you were making those potatoes and fried chicken for the dinner."

"Hold on." Carmella got up and rushed to the kitchen. She figured it would be better to show them, than to try to convince them that vegetables could be just as delicious as starchy potatoes. She warmed the plates she had made earlier in the microwave and then took them out to the girls. "Here's one for you." She put the plate in front of Renee. "And one for you." She handed the other plate to Joy.

"Mmm, this is good. And you're right, it does taste like au gratin potatoes," Renee said.

"This turkey is good, too."

Sitting back down, Carmella said. "So, spaghetti squash, turkey and green beans. Does that sound like something you'd be okay with at your rehearsal dinner?"

"I don't mind eating light. Jay will probably thank you, especially since it will help me keep my figure... "Well, at least until I have a few kids."

"You'll be able to keep your figure even after you and Jay have children. Just eat right and exercise," Carmella told her.

"Is that what you're doing? Because it looks like you've lost some weight," Joy said.

"You noticed?" Carmella was grinning from ear to ear as she stood up and turned to the left and then back around. "I've lost ten pounds."

"Good for you. I'm on board," Joy said, and then asked, "What's for dessert?"

Turning to Renee for approval, Carmella said, "I was thinking that we could do a sugar-free chocolate pudding in a glass that we would fill with whip cream and strawberries."

"Sounds yummy. And I bet it will look even better than it will taste," Renee said.

"I think we can pretty it up. Don't you worry. Just leave it to me," Carmella told her.

"Okay, what gives, Mom? During my wedding sugar and carbs were flowing like milk and honey. Why are you changing things up for Renee's wedding?"

She'd just about had Renee convinced about accepting the lighter fare, but now that Joy had opened her question-everything-mouth, Renee just might change her mind. No matter the outcome, Carmella wasn't upset with Joy. Her daughter's personality was what made her an awesome attorney. "The older I get the more I wonder if I've made the right decisions in the foods I feed my family. I want you all to live long, happy and healthy lives. So, Ramsey and I have made changes in the way we eat. And I just wanted to share some of that with all of you... It's all in love."

"Everything you do is in love, Mom," Joy said as she leaned over and hugged Carmella.

Renee joined in on the hug. "I love you, Mama Carmella, and I love your menu idea. Let's do it."

***

There was a shift in the air. RaShawn Thomas felt it and wondered what God was up to. He had gone the distance, doing whatever was required of him during the

36

seven years he'd spent as a missionary in numerous countries. But this last mission had taken a toll on him. For about six months now, RaShawn had been wondering if he was truly where God wanted him. He hadn't seen his family in five years and hadn't been able to develop any lasting relationships.

This morning he picked up his mail from the post office and almost shed a tear when he read the Christmas card from his dad and Mama Carmella. It wasn't so much the Christmas card that saddened RaShawn but the note Mama Carmella attached to it. From what she wrote, RaShawn gathered that all of his brothers were bailing on Christmas with the family and choosing to spend it with their in-laws this year.

His father loved having his family around during the holidays; Carmella loved it even more, so he knew that they weren't taking their new reality very well. But then again, they did have Renee's wedding to worry about... another family wedding that he was going to miss.

"Dr. RaShawn, come quickly. It's Chima's time."
***

Brielle bounced up and down in her highchair as Maxine took the sugar cookies out of the oven. She turned to her daughter and said, "I hope you don't think you're getting any of these cookies."

"Want cookie. Want cookie," Brielle chanted as she continued bouncing up and down and banging on the table top of her highchair.

"I have to decorate these cookies so Daddy can take them to his Christmas party at work."

"That's right. I need those cookies for work," Ramsey said as he entered the kitchen with his cell phone pressed against his ear. "You know you're not right, Ronny. Dontae and I will be with the Dawson family on Christmas, watching Dontae explain why his and Jewel's first child was named after Mama Carmella rather than Jewel's mother." Ramsey chuckled and then said, "So you know that Mama Carmella and Daddy want you to come home."

After several beats of silence while he listened to Ronny, Ramsey said, "Am I talking to Ronny Thomas or President Obama, because ain't nobody as busy as you but the President of the good ol' US of A."

"Want cookie, Daddy."

"Of course you do, my little princess." Ramsey took one of the cookies off of the cookie sheet and handed it to Brielle. She beamed up at him as if he was responsible for hanging the moon.

Father and daughter looked so cute together. Watching them play and laugh normally brought a smile to Maxine's face, but today she wasn't in the mood. "I hope you plan to brush her teeth after filling her full of sugar." Maxine untied her apron, threw it on the counter and rushed out of the kitchen.

By the time she made it to their bedroom, Maxine was feeling ashamed of her actions. She had been rude to Ramsey for reasons that had nothing to do with his giving Brielle a cookie. She got on her knees and lowered her head as she prayed to the Lord. "I'm so sorry for being angry and miserable lately, but You know the desires of my heart, Lord. You know that I am so grateful that I get to be a mother to a child of Ramsey's seed. But I want more children and since my body won't produce them, then I'm begging you, God, give me a baby. Thank You, Lord Jesus, thank You."

Tears were streaming down Maxine's face as Ramsey opened the bedroom door with Brielle in his arms. He quickly put Brielle down as he saw his wife sobbing on the floor. Ramsey bent down and put his arms around her. He didn't know what to say to comfort her, all he could do was hold her and be there for her.

"Thank You, Jesus," Maxine said again.

"Are you all right, Mommy?" Brielle asked, touching Maxine's head.

With her free arm, Maxine pulled Brielle into their embrace. She kissed her little girl's head, and tried to reassure the child of her love. With everything in

Maxine, she dearly loved Brielle. She wished that the child Ramsey had with another woman was enough for her, but Maxine wanted to give Brielle a brother or sister. *God, please help me*, was her silent plea.

Chapter 5

"Ramsey, oh my goodness, come see," Carmella called from their bedroom.

Ramsey came into the room holding a tray. He set an egg white omelet with spinach, tomatoes, onions, green peppers and shredded cheese in front of his wife. "For my queen."

She kissed him. "Thank you, baby, this looks so good I can't wait to eat it. But first I want to show you something." Carmella lifted her blood glucose meter. The numbers displayed on the screen were 136.

Ramsey took a flying leap off the bed and shouted right in the middle of their bedroom floor. He didn't need music or a church building to get his shout on. "God is so good. I can't believe that your numbers have come down a hundred points." He rushed back over to his wife and kissed her again. "I'm a believer now... you're healed. I'm just sorry that I doubted God in the first place."

Carmella lifted a hand. "I believe God and I know that I will be healed, but I don't want to keep anything from you. Even though that number is a hundred times better than where I was first thing in the morning several weeks ago, it's still too high and considered a diabetic number."

Ramsey sat back, a little deflated. "Then why did you show it to me?"

"Because Ramsey, I believe that we are on the right track. I've been exercising with you twice a week and taking long walks at least two other days a week, while still eating right and God is rewarding us by letting us see progress."

"Progress is good, but I want to see an end to this disease. I don't want you sick or living with the threat of kidney or heart problems."

"I received a good report from the eye doctor yesterday. She said I'm far sighted and my age is what has caused my recent eyesight problems. She saw no trace of diabetes in my eyes."

"Praise the Lord!"

"Well, we were going to do that anyhow, but isn't it awesome to have some good news to praise Him for?"

***

"She's going in and out of consciousness, Dr. RaShawn. What do I do?" the young midwife asked.

RaShawn was more terrified than he let on. Chima had been displaying signs of high blood pressure and preeclampsia for the last three months of her pregnancy. He'd done everything he could to help her, but nothing seemed to work. All he could do now was pray. "Don't pass out on us, Chima. I need you to push. Come on, let's get this baby delivered and then you can take a nice long rest. I promise you."

Chima's eyes fluttered and seemed to roll back in her head. RaShawn shook her. "Stay with me, Chima. Come on, push."

At that moment Chima seemed to find strength enough to pull herself up and grab hold of Dr. RaShawn's arm. "Name her Abeni, because me and my husband, we asked for her."

"Push her out and you'll be able to name her yourself," RaShawn tried to encourage.

"And promise me that you'll take her to America, and find another family that has asked for her also... do you hear me? There's another family out there that wants Abeni even more than I do."

"I hear you, now push."

Chima laid back down. She let out a loud, horrible scream as she pushed one final time. As the baby came out of her, Chima went limp.

Holding the baby in his arms, RaShawn lifted his eyes to heaven. "What am I supposed to do now, God?" The baby's father had died five months ago, after a hurricane had ravaged the town. He felt Chima's pulse... nothing.

Through tears, RaShawn smiled down at the baby and said, "I guess we'll call you Abeni."

***

"I don't like what this is doing to us," Lance said as he sat across from his wife at the dining room table.

"I just don't understand why you get so upset over the fact that I'm not ready to have kids yet." Joy wished she could avoid this conversation for a few more years, but it was not to be.

"We've been married for seven years. How much more time do you need?"

"I'm worried about losing ground, Lance. How many judges do you know who have to play PTA mom or someone who has to leave work early to go pick up the kids?"

Lance shook his head. "Don't you think that being a wife and mother can be more rewarding than any judicial position you could ever obtain?"

She wanted to say yes. Just tell Lance that she'd give anything to have his children and be a mother to them. But images appeared in her mind of her mother falling apart after her father left her when she still had two kids to take care of. Joy would not give up her job and become a homemaker while Lance went out into the world and became some big success. She remembered how her mother always stood in the background cheering Nelson Marshall to victory.

But her father never appreciated all the things her mother did to make their home into precisely what he wanted it to be. Joy's deepest fear was that Lance would one day take her for granted, and stop seeing her worth.

"What's the real problem, Joy? Tell me something, because I am beginning to lose faith that we will ever have a family."

She leaned over and let her fingers trail down his chin. "You're so handsome, how could I not want to have kids with you?"

"I'm not in the mood to joke around, Joy. I really want this. Tell me why you don't."

Sighing, Joy closed her eyes, asked the Lord to walk her through this moment in time. Then, as she opened her eyes again, Joy admitted, "It's not that I don't want to have children with you, but every time I think about it, fear clinches my heart."

"What are you so afraid of, baby? Don't you know that I'll be here for you and our baby?"

When she didn't respond to that, Lance said, "I'm serious. I know that you still want to work. That's not a problem for me. We could even get a nanny if that would make things easier."

"And you would approve of me hiring a nanny to help me out with our children so I could continue working?"

"If it would make you happy."

Lance was so good to her. Once, when she'd had a problem with him representing a client who had harmed Dontae, Lance had turned the case down, even though taking the case would have boosted his career, he still walked away from it because she had asked him to. How could she continue to deny him, when she knew in her heart that he wouldn't deny her anything?

Chapter 6

Renee made up her mind. She wouldn't allow Marlin to have another minute of her life. She was going to go to the Bahamas with Jay and enjoy her honeymoon. The Bahamas was a beautiful place and beautiful things happened to her while she was over there. She'd gone to church and given her life to the Lord and she and Jay had fallen in love there... she would simply put that other event out of her mind. It was an outlier.

"My bags are packed," she told Jay as they stood at the altar practicing their wedding vows.

Smiling at the news, Jay responded to the officiant and said, "I do."

Raven hugged her younger sister, Renee as she stepped down from the altar. "You two look so much in love. I'm happy for you."

Renee squeezed her sister real tight as she whispered in her ear, "I'm sorry that you have to be a bridesmaid again, but don't worry. I will soon be a bridesmaid for you."

"I just wish I knew where he's been hiding," Raven said as they walked out of the church.

After the practice everyone went back to her dad's and Mama Carmella's house for the rehearsal dinner. Even though Mama Carmella didn't have her traditional Christmas cookies on tables all around the house, she had decorated the house. This year all the bulbs, flowers and ribbons were either burgundy or gold to match Renee's wedding colors.

"It looks beautiful in here," Renee told Carmella. "Why didn't you tell me that you were doing this? I would have come over to help you put all of these decorations up."

Carmella waved the thought away. "Your dad hired a decorator. I didn't have to lift a finger."

Looking around the room, Dontae said, "Mom, I don't believe that you let someone else decorate this house for Christmas... well and the wedding party, too. When we were kids you wouldn't even let *us* help you."

"You just hand me my grandbaby and stay out of my business," Carmella told her son as she lifted baby Cammie out of his arms. Hugging the baby tightly, Carmella added, "I'm so glad you and Jewel were able to come to the wedding so I could finally see my namesake in person."

"Yeah, Mom, why didn't you go to Charlotte when they had the baby?" Joy asked. "I kept expecting you to ask me to ride shotgun."

"Like you would have gone." Carmella gave her daughter a look that said, don't even go there.

"Well, I do have a huge caseload, but I'm not the grandmother and the baby isn't named after me."

"Stop starting trouble, Joy," Ramsey said as he joined the group. "Your mom and I have had a lot on our plate recently. But we are planning a week-long visit to Charlotte in the very near future."

Carmella handed the baby to Joy. "You just hold my grandbaby while I get the table ready for our meal."

Cammie started to cry as she was being passed from her grandmother to her aunt. Joy rocked her and sang to her. The baby started cooing and blowing little baby bubbles. Joy felt eyes on her, and looked up to see Lance standing in the back or the room staring at her as if the sight of her with a child in her arms brought pure joy to his heart. She tried to turn away from him, but their eyes locked and held.

Dontae came up behind Joy and took his daughter out of her arms. "You and your husband look like you're plotting to steal my baby. Y'all need to go make one of your own."

"Shut up, goof ball, don't nobody want to steal something that poops and spits up. I'll wait until you and Jewel potty train her, then you might have something to fear from me."

"You do know that diapers and throw up cloths are available for all babies, right? So you might as well go into baby training by changing as many of Brielle's diapers as possible."

Joy had been smiling, enjoying the banter with her brother, but after he mentioned baby training the smile left her face. She grabbed hold of Dontae's arm. "Can I talk to you for a minute?"

"Sure sis, what's up?"

She pushed him towards the kitchen. And while he played with and gazed at Cammie, only half listening to her, Joy said, "How did you do it?"

"Huh? Do what?" Dontae finally took his eyes off the baby and looked at his sister.

"I'm scared to death of having kids and then having my family bust up. But you don't seem to be worried about that at all. I need you to give me whatever you've been smoking so I can finally make my husband just as happy as you are."

Dontae leaned his head back and laughed. He then put a hand on Joy's shoulder and said, "Let me tell you a little secret... I still had doubts about happily ever after even while Jewel and I were headed to the hospital to have Cammie. But the minute I held my baby in my arms all the fear went away. She and my wife are the best things that ever happened to me. And I will be in her life for as long as I live."

"That's easy to say now, but what if you get the itch like Daddy did after twenty-three years of marriage?"

"Then shame on him," Jewel said as she walked over to Joy and Dontae. She then reached out her hands and said, "I think she needs to be changed."

"I can do that," Dontae said as he leaned over and kissed Jewel. Then he kissed Joy on the cheek and said, "Diaper duty calls, I must hurry."

"He's so silly," Jewel said as she watched her husband put Cammie under his arm like a football and pretend to be running for a touchdown. She sighed, "Some days I think he really misses playing football."

"Not as much as he loves you and Cammie."

"Oh I know that. My man loves me and I love him right back."

"I wish I was more like you, Jewel. But then again, your parents are still together so you have a perfect example of love lasting forever."

Jewel put her hands on Joy's shoulder and turned her to face Carmella and Ramsey. They were in the middle of a kiss as they stood under the mistletoe. "So do you. If I remember the story correctly, those two loved each other since they were teenagers. They may have had their time apart, but they will be together until the end. I have no doubt of that."

* * *

Family and friends sat down to enjoy a scrumptious meal before Renee said her vows and left for the Bahamas the next day. Conversation was flowing as the food was being passed from hand to hand and then being scooped out of the bowls and put on each plate. The spaghetti squash casserole, green beans, mashed cauliflower and turkey and gravy. As each person began to taste the food, questions started swirling around the table.

"Ma, these mashed potatoes are good, but it's something different about them," Dontae said as he continued to eat.

"I used cauliflower instead of potatoes," Carmella told him, smiling, clearly proud of the food she put on the table.

Ram pointed at a section of his plate. "This kind of tastes like au gratin potatoes, but I know it's not because of all the shredded stuff in it."

"That shredded stuff," Ramsey Sr. said as he laughed at his son, "is spaghetti squash."

"Not bad," Maxine said. "You'll have to give me this recipe. I've been trying to eat healthier, but I only know about two or three different things to fix."

"Ramsey and I are planning to come visit you all in a few weeks, I'll bring some recipes and you and I can get in the kitchen."

"Count me in," Jewel said. "I want to learn how to fix healthier food as well."

"Hold on now," Dontae said, "I'm a red meat and potatoes man. You can't be feeding me these vegetables all the time."

"You'll live longer, so we're doing it." Jewel turned back to Carmella. "Like I said, count me in."

"Jay, wouldn't you like me to fix some of these recipes. I want you to be healthy and live a long time, so that we can enjoy our life together."

Chowing down on the meal, Jay finished chewing his food and said, "Sure thing, baby."

"What do you think he's going to say," Dontae interjected. "The man is getting married tomorrow; he's not trying to make any waves until the honeymoon is over."

After dinner, Dontae and Ramsey stood together whispering about the meal. "Everything was good, but something just ain't right. Where was the mac and cheese... where was the sweet potatoes?"

"I feel you, Dontae, but Mama Carmella and Daddy are getting older. Maybe they just want to be healthier."

"Something don't smell right here. And I'm going to find out what's going on." Dontae gathered his brothers and sisters in the family room and said, "We need to find out what's going on with Mama and Ramsey."

"Why do you think something is going on?" Raven asked.

"I know my mother. She has never been concerned about whether or not there were enough vegetables on the plate. And did any of you notice that there are no cookies around the house? She normally has dozens of cookies made by this time of year. Each table would have a plate of cookies on it."

"I didn't think much of it. But she wouldn't even share the donuts she made for me at her bakery. She was sipping on a protein shake instead," Joy told the group.

Carmella and Ramsey walked into the family room and stepped in the middle of the conversation. Renee quickly asked, "Why are there no cookies?"

"Huh?" Ramsey Sr. looked surprised by the question. "I thought you all enjoyed the dinner."

"We did. Mama can cook anything and make it taste good, but that's not the point," Dontae said, then

54

added, "I know something is wrong, and I want to know what's going on."

Chapter 7

"Sit down," Carmella said to her children as she and Ramsey held hands. "We need to tell you all what's been going on."

"You're sick, aren't you?" Dontae's hands went up in the air as he strutted back and forth, rubbing his forehead. "I knew something was wrong when you didn't come to see Cammie."

"Dontae, please sit down and let me explain." Ramsey squeezed Carmella's hand as she said, "The doctors say I'm sick. But I'm telling you that I'm healed. The Lord that I serve has healed me."

"What's wrong, Mama. Will you at least tell us that?" Joy asked, fear gathering in her eyes.

"At least let us know what we need to be praying about. It's not fair to keep us in the dark like this. Because I'm really not in the mood to lose another mother," Ram said.

"You're not going to lose me. The doctors say that I have diabetes. They said that my numbers were so high that I could have had a heart attack or a stroke."

"But they have medication to fix diabetes, right?" Renee asked.

Carmella shook her head. "The medication the doctors offer for diabetes does not cure the disease. It may help moderate your blood sugar, but I worry about what it does to the body in the long term, so I've decided not to take any medication."

"What?" the room exploded with objections from each of their children.

Ramsey lifted a hand to quiet the group. "Hear your mother out, please."

"I truly believe that diabetes is a lifestyle disease. I have thoroughly researched the matter and I believe that my cure lies in the very foods that God has blessed this world with. So, Ramsey and I are now eating more vegetables like spinach and broccoli and lean proteins. I've started working out and I feel better now than I have in months."

"But are you monitoring your blood sugar levels? That's really nothing to play with," Jewel said.

"Yes, hon, I monitor it daily. I'm also working with a dietician and seeing my doctor regularly."

"Okay." Dontae came to stand in front of his mother. "Since you're telling us that you're not going to take medication and that you've been healed, I want to see proof. Have your blood sugar levels come down? Show us the proof of this miracle."

Carmella turned to her husband. "Would you get the tablet I've been recording my blood glucose reading on?" Then she turned back to her son and said, "I don't appreciate your sarcasm, but since I know you are worried about me, I'm going to let it go this time."

"No disrespect meant at all, Mama. I just don't want you sick."

She gently touched her son's face as she said, "I'm doing better, so stop worrying."

Ramsey came back into the room. "Here it is." He set the paper on the table.

Carmella pointed to the top of the page. "When I first started keeping track my blood sugar levels, they were staying at around 230 every morning."

"What is it supposed to be at?" Lance asked as he looked over Joy's shoulder at Carmella's log.

"Non-diabetic people are below 100."

Raven pointed at the paperwork and then said, "Yesterday it was 123. What does that means?"

"It means that I've come down over a hundred points. But if I stay at that level, then I am considered pre-diabetic. My goal is to totally reverse diabetes. So, I won't be satisfied until I see below 100 numbers on a consistent basis."

"You know what, Mama? Dontae mentioned the fact that we don't have cookies this year, but if it means that you are living a healthier life, I don't ever need you to make any more cookies," Joy told her.

"I'd like to make you all a promise," Carmella said. "If my blood sugar level drops below 100 on Christmas, I will spend the day baking cookies and then Ramsey and I will mail each of you a box. But I don't want you eating all those cookies... take a few and then share the rest with friends. I want all of us to start thinking about eating healthy and indulging in sweets in moderation. Okay?"

"I know it sounds strange that Carmella has now become the sugar police. Especially since we own a bakery full of sugary goods." Ramsey smiled at Carmella as he continued, "But just so you all know, we have decided to sell the bakery."

"But you love Hallelujah Cakes and Such," Renee interjected, "How can you just let it go so easily?"

Smiling, showing that she was okay with the decision, Carmella said, "Getting healthy is one thing. But Ramsey and I want to ensure that I stay healthy. And all that sugar and flour is just not good for us on a day in and day out basis. I just don't want those everyday temptations in my life anymore."

***

Renee and Jay's wedding was beautiful, and the reception hall had been decorated to perfection. Everyone loved the French vanilla cake with all of its gold and burgundy flowers on top of each layer. The guests were eating, dancing and having a good time at the reception.

However, Ram and Dontae couldn't get into the festivities. They were too busy watching Carmella and thinking about everything that transpired the night before. "I don't like it. She's over there laughing and acting like she's having a good time, but who knows how she's really feeling."

"I just wish she would take the medicine. That would make me feel better about leaving her here while we head back to Charlotte," Ram told Dontae.

Dontae's eyes widened as if inspiration had just hit him, he then told Ram, "I think I know what we need to do; we just need to convince the wives."

"What do you need to convince your wife of?" Jewel asked as she came up behind Dontae.

Dontae swung around, looked at his wife as if she was the loveliest vision he'd ever seen. "I can hardly believe how good you look in that dress. Girl, you better get on that dance floor with me, so I can show you off."

"You really like my dress?" Jewel twirled around. "I worried that my stomach wasn't flat enough yet."

"Jewel, please, I can't even tell by looking at you that you had a baby three weeks ago. I might as well hurry up and have a brother for Cammie because being pregnant obviously doesn't bother you at all."

"Nice try," Jewel said as she grabbed his arm and pulled him towards the dance floor. "Hopefully you can dance without thinking about getting me pregnant."

Ram laughed at Jewel's comment. But it was a bittersweet kind of laugh because Ram wanted to give Maxine the world, but the truth was, the one thing that she wanted, was the only thing he couldn't make happen for her.

***

"What are you going to do with this baby? You have no wife and you don't even have a stable home since you travel from country to country."

RaShawn knew that Erline, his nurse was only thinking of him with her comment, but RaShawn felt God in this new situation he found himself in. Abeni was a part of his life for a reason bigger than RaShawn could comprehend, but when God was up to something, RaShawn knew enough to get out of the way and let God do what He wanted to do. He told Erline, "The way I see this is that Chima wanted me to make sure that her baby went to someone who really wanted her, and if the African council approves, I'm going to take Abeni home with me and ask my family to help me with this task."

"Just as long as you aren't thinking of keeping her for yourself. As young and handsome as you are, you don't need to be strapped down by a baby. You need to get out there and find a wife so you can have a bunch of children yourself."

"I'm only twenty-nine, what's the rush?"

Shaking her head, Erline told him, "I think you're just scared of falling in love. That's why you have such wanderlust. Flying from one continent to another. Yeah, you've been doing a great service, but you've also been running from love, and I'd like to know why?"

RaShawn picked up Abeni and said, "Maybe I've got all the love I need right here."

Erline took Abeni out of his arms and as she began walking out the room with her, she said, "You better hope they let you keep this baby."

That was the thing RaShawn worried most about. He had a feeling that God already had a family in mind for Abeni; he just had to get her to them. But if he was denied a travel visa for the baby, then they both were going to be stuck here for Christmas.

Chapter 8

Joy's phone rang at 6 a.m. on Christmas morning. She was tempted to just let it go to voicemail, but she checked the caller ID and saw that it was Renee. Since Renee and Jay were in the Bahamas on their honeymoon, Joy figured something must have happened for her to be calling so early. She sat up in bed and answered her phone. "Hey honeymooner, what's got you up so early?"

"I could hardly sleep last night," Renee said in a whisper.

"Does that mean Jay stayed up all night with you?" Joy's voice was full of merriment.

"You are a funny girl. But if you must know, we are very much enjoying our honeymoon and have decided to extend our stay in the Bahamas for an extra week... but I can't stay if Mama Carmella isn't doing better. So, I'm calling to see if you know what her numbers were yesterday?"

"She wouldn't tell me. But I'm getting ready to get up and go over there this morning. Remember, she said that if her blood sugar levels were below 100 today, she would be up baking cookies all day. I plan to help her bake as many cookies as she desires."

"Send me and Jay a box to our hotel."

"First thing in the morning," Joy said as she flung off the covers.

"Listen to us, we sound like we actually believe in miracles or something. You do know that most doctors don't believe that diabetes can be reversed," Renee said.

"Most doctors don't know the God that Carmella Marshall-Thomas serves."

"The God we all serve," Renee said and then added, "I have been praying like never before that God would move this thing out of Mama Carmella's life."

"I think we've all been praying... well, most of us, we still have a few in this family who don't realize that God answers prayers."

"Once Mama Carmella is walking in total healing, maybe we should get a prayer chain going for my knuckleheaded brother, Ronnie. I still can't believe he wouldn't take two seconds from his career to come to my wedding."

"He'll come to his senses," Joy assured Renee, then said, "I'll call you back when I get to the house and see what Mama is up to."

***

Raven had taken two weeks off work so she could spend time with her family. As she got out of bed that morning, her mind spiraled back to when she was ten years old and went into her parents' bedroom and watched as her mother threw up blood into the toilet. Not long after that day, her dad had come home from the hospital and told all of them that they wouldn't be seeing their mother ever again, because she had died.

Standing at her father's and Carmella's bedroom door, Raven wanted to knock on it and ask Carmella what her test results were this morning, but she was afraid to ask. Then the doorbell downstairs rang and it gave her an excuse to do something else... anything else but discover whether her mother of the last ten years was healthy or not.

***

As Carmella opened her eyes that morning, she felt a sense of unease kick her in the gut. Why had she given her children a date for when she expected her numbers to normalize? Why hadn't she just she said that it would happen sometime in the near future and not given them a day to look forward to? Joy had called and asked about her numbers yesterday and she had changed the subject, because when she had tested she had been at 112. Which was good, but not good enough to prove to her children that she no longer had to worry about all the horrible ways in which diabetes can wreak havoc in her life.

She looked over at the blood glucose meter that she kept on her dresser and dreaded the thought of checking her levels this morning. Carmella knew in her heart, mind, body and spirit that God was working this thing out for her. She just didn't know the day or the hour it would be worked out, so she never should have given her children false hope, especially on a day like Christmas.

Closing her eyes, she said a quick prayer, asking God for the healing that He had already promised to give to her when Jesus was wounded on the cross.

Fear not, Carmella, God has heard your prayers and He has healed you.

Carmella tapped Ramsey on the shoulder, "Did you just hear that?"

"Hear what?" Ramsey asked, struggling to get his eyes opened.

"Nether mind, go back to sleep," Carmella said as she got out of bed and quickly made her way to her bathroom and shut the door. She then danced for the Lord as quietly as she could. Because she had just heard the voice of an angel right in her bedroom, in the midst of her doubt and wavering. But Carmella wasn't wavering about the situation anymore. Just as soon as she finished giving praise to God, she opened that bathroom door and boldly strutted back into her bedroom. She sat down her the bed, took out her equipment, did what she had to do, and then sat back and waited on the blood glucose reading to show up on the monitor. The machine beeped and within one, two, three beats, the monitor read 98.

Carmella started screaming, she shook Ramsey. This time, he sat up, "What's wrong?"

"Look baby... just look."

Carmella put the meter in his face and as Ramsey saw the two-digit reading, his eyes filled with tears and he began worshiping God for His goodness.

The bedroom door burst open, Raven and Joy rushed in, terror etched across their faces.

"Merry Christmas, you two," Carmella said.

"I thought something was wrong. I heard screaming," Raven said.

"No, hon, nothing is wrong. In fact, everything is all right." Carmella lifted the glucose meter and showed the reading to her children, then they joined Ramsey in praise to God while Carmella sat back down on the edge of her bed, lifted her head heavenward and simply said, "Thank You."

"I guess we need to get started baking those cookies," Joy said as they finished their praise party.

"Where is Lance?" Carmella asked.

"He's still asleep."

"Girl, you better get back home with my son-in-law and start your Christmas morning with him."

"He'll be over here after he drops a few presents off to his parents. I'm here to help because I know for a fact that all of my brothers and sisters are going to be looking for a cookie delivery this week."

Smiling, Carmella said, "Let's head to the kitchen, then. I'll make you all my famous egg white spinach omelet and then we'll start baking the cookies."

"You are really embracing this new way of eating, aren't you Mama Carmella?" Raven asked as her father put his arms around her and they headed downstairs.

"I'm actually excited about it. I have so much more energy and I feel better since cutting sugar and white carbs out of my diet."

"She's made a believer out of me," Ramsey said, while patting his stomach. "I've taken twenty-five pounds off since we changed our eating habits."

Carmella rolled her eyes. "Don't that just prove that life isn't fair? While my weight loss is inching along, he's dropping pounds like it's nothing."

Chapter 9

Lance arrived an hour after the cookie baking began. Joy kissed her husband and then handed him a rolling pin. All hands were needed in the kitchen today because Carmella was feeling ambitious and had decided to make ten different kinds of cookies, from sugar, chocolate chip, and snicker doodle to macadamia nut with white chocolate chips. But no one seemed to mind, the kitchen was full of laugher and joy.

"I can't believe that I'm going to be giving this up pretty soon," Carmella said, as she looked at all the bowls and cookie sheets that lined the tables and counters.

"Are you sure that you really want to sell the bakery? You've worked so hard and built that business from the ground up," Joy said.

Carmella nodded. "It's time. My husband and I have decided that we are going to spend the rest of our time on earth worshiping God, traveling and babysitting our grandbabies."

Joy looked up to see if Lance's eyes were on her and they were. She gave him a quick smile and then got back to stirring her cookie dough.

As they were putting another batch of cookies in the oven the doorbell rang. "I wonder who that is." She turned to Ramsey and asked, "We weren't expecting anyone else for Christmas, were we?"

He shook his head. "The boys are scattered this year and Renee is in the Bahamas."

"That reminds me," Joy said as she pulled her cell phone out of her purse. "I was supposed to call Renee to tell her what your glucose reading was this morning."

Carmella wiped her hands. "Since nobody else is heading towards the door, I guess I'll get it." Carmella's eyes misted as she saw the five people who were standing on her porch. Opening the door, she said, "I thought you all were staying in Charlotte this year?"

"Now you know we weren't going to stay away from those cookies you promised us," Dontae said as he bent down and kissed his mother on the cheek and then handed her the present that was in his hands.

"You take that present to the living room and put it under the tree. I want to hold my grandbaby."

Jewel, Ram and Maxine stepped into the house as Jewel put Cammie in Carmella's arms.

"Ram, don't tell me that you're only here for the cookies, too?" Carmella asked teasingly.

"I'm not even going to front, Mama Carmella. We couldn't take being away from you this Christmas, so we spent Christmas Eve with the Dawson family and got on the highway first thing this morning."

Carmella gave Ram and Maxine one armed hugs and then sat down with the baby and took Cammie's coat off. "I'm so happy to have you all here. I didn't want to be selfish, because I know that you boys are married now," she said to Ram and Dontae, but I'm thankful that I get my boys home this year."

"We knew these two big babies wouldn't be able to handle Christmas without their mommy this year, so Maxine and I compromised," Jewel said.

"So tell us, Mama Carmella," Maxine chimed in. "I already smell the cookies, so I know it's good news, but what was your reading this morning?"

"98."

"Hot dog," Dontae said as he and Ram high-fived. "This means you're getting better, right?"

"As far as I'm concerned, it means I'm healed and I intend to stay that way. So, you all need to get to that kitchen and eat up those cookies, because I'm not touching them."

Not long after the first batch of cookies was dusted off, the doorbell rang again. This time Ramsey opened the door to see his way-too-busy son, Ronnie on the other side of the door. "Well, aren't you a sight for sore eyes. Get in here, boy."

"I can't stay long, Dad. I just came to drop off presents and to see Mama Carmella for myself. I know that you said she's doing better, but I just have to see it for myself."

Ramsey nodded. "I understand, son. Come in. We're happy for whatever time you can give us today." As they entered the kitchen, Ramsey said, "Hey everybody, look what the wind blew in."

Shouts of joy went up all around the room. For this was a family that truly loved one another, and wished for nothing but the best for one another.

As Carmella stood back and watched her family laugh and joke with each other as they passed cookie trays around, she thought to herself that there was one thing that would make this day absolutely perfect for her. But when the doorbell rang again, she never imagined that her fondest wish would be standing on the other side of the door.

But as tears streamed down her face, she opened the door and welcomed RaShawn back home. "God is so good. I was just wishing that you were here." She tried to hug him, but it was a bit awkward with the bundle he carried.

"Hold on," RaShawn said, "Let me put the baby down so I can give you a proper hug.

"What baby?" Carmella asked as she took the bundle out of his arms. She unwrapped the bundle and as she came face to face with a beautiful baby girl, she squealed with joy. "Whose child is this, RaShawn?"

Before he could answer the rest of the family came out of the kitchen and joined them in the foyer. Ramsey rushed over to his son and gave him a hug that tried to make up for the seven years' worth of hugs they had missed.

"I can't believe it. My baby boy has come home."

The rest of the family took turns hugging RaShawn and introducing him to his new sisters-in-law.

"Come on everyone, let's go in the living room and open presents. But I'm telling y'all right now; I don't need anything. Having my family here is present enough for me," Carmella said as she led the way to the living room.

Maxine took the baby out of Carmella's arms as they began passing presents around the room. But Maxine wasn't thinking about the gifts under the tree, she was too busy being captivated by the baby in her arms.

Brielle cozied up to her and asked, "Mommy, who are you holding?"

"I think she's RaShawn's daughter," Maxine told her.

RaShawn's head popped up. "She's not mine. I delivered her just before her mother passed away. She asked me to name her Abeni, which means, we asked for her. And just before she died, she told me that another family was out there who also asked for Abeni; she wanted me to find them."

"You're kidding right?" Maxine turned from RaShawn to Ram and then back to RaShawn. "I have been praying, asking God for another child. I can't have any of my own, but I would love this little girl like my own if she were mine."

Ram got up from his spot beside the tree. He stood next to his wife and looked down at the precious bundle in her arms. He then turned to his brother. "Are you serious, RaShawn? Are you truly looking for a family for this little girl?"

RaShawn nodded. "I believe God directed me home for the purpose of finding Abeni a home with parents who will love her like she belonged to them."

With the baby in her arms, Maxine stood and hugged Ram. "She's supposed to be ours, Ram, I feel it in my heart. She already belongs to me." Maxine bent down and kissed Brielle's cheek; as she stood back up she said, "I know just as I knew Brielle was meant for me from the moment I saw her. God must have put a yearning in my heart for another child, so that we would be ready to receive Abeni when she was delivered to us."

"I think she's right, Ram. I know God directed me here. And from what you all told me a month ago, you and Maxine weren't even supposed to be here today."

Ram put a hand on his brother's shoulder and said, "Thank you for this gift, RaShawn. We'll fill out whatever paperwork is necessary for Abeni to become ours."

Once Ram said that the room filled with holiday cheer. It was Christmas and the spirit of giving and loving others more than yourself was spreading.

Joy walked over to her husband, holding a jewelry box. She sat down next to her husband and handed it to him.

"Jewelry, you shouldn't have," Lance said and meant it, because that was not the kind of gift that he wanted from his wife.

"Open it." She nudged him.

Lance set the box next to him and told her, "I'll open it later."

Joy stood with hands on hips. She turned to her family and said, "I need y'all's help. Come over here and help me encourage my husband to open the present I gave him."

The family joined Joy and began chanting, "Open it, open it, open it!"

"All right already," Lance said as he grabbed the box and started tearing the wrapping paper off of it. "If it's so important to you, then I will open it now." He took the lid off the box and as his eyes narrowed in on the pregnancy test, he turned to Joy and asked, "W-what does this mean?"

"We're pregnant!" Joy shouted as Lance stood up and hugged her.

"Oh my goodness, do you know what this means, Ramsey?" Carmella asked.

"What?"

"We might have to postpone our trip to Greece that you planned for next year. I have to be right here to see this grandchild come into the world."

"Instead of postponing it, maybe I'll just take you there next week. We'll bring in our New Year traveling, just as we've always dreamed about doing."

"You've got a deal." Carmella was the happiest woman in the world on this Christmas. She had her health, three grandchildren in the house and another on the way, but most of all, her family knew what it's like to have God in their lives and that was truly the best gift of all.

The End.

You have been reading Praise for Christmas which is the sixth book in the Praise Him Anyhow Series. If you'd like to know more about the Marshall-Thomas family and find out why certain things occurred in this Christmas Novella, you may want to read the other books in the series. I recommend starting with book 1 (Tears Fall at Night).

Excerpt of Book 7

His Love Walk

by

Vanessa Miller

Prologue

Carmella Marshall-Thomas woke up in a cold sweat. She shook her husband until he woke up and sat up next to her in the bed. "I just had a nightmare. Ronny was dead."

"What?" Ramsey turned on the light next to their bed.

"I'm scared, Ramsey. The last time I felt like this Renee was being stalked and she and Jay almost lost their lives."

Rubbing his chin as he focused on his wife of the last fifteen years, Ramsey tried to sound calm. "I've studied a little about dreams. Tell me this, did you see blood?"

"No, there was no blood. Is seeing blood bad?"

Sighing in relief, Ramsey said, "Let's just say, it wouldn't be good. At least some dream interpreters don't think so. Now tell me about the dream."

"It was kind of weird. I went to Ronny's house because I was angry that we hadn't seen him in a while." Shaking her head, Carmella said, "That boy works entirely too hard. I mean, I know he desires success, but how much of it does he need?"

"Carmella, can you please get back to your dream?"

"I'm sorry, but Ronny and I used to be so close, and now..." she trailed off as she thought about how long it had been since Ronny had bothered to come home for a visit. Even though Ronny was already grown by the time she married his father, Carmella still thought of all five of Ramsey's children as if they were just like the two she'd conceived with her first husband. They all belonged to her. They were her children and she would worry about the things that concerned them until the good Lord took her home.

Ramsey wiped a tear from her face as he said, "He's a grown man, honey, we've got to move out of the way and let him live his life."

"But the women in the dream told me he was dead."

"What women?"

"Women were everywhere. I kept trying to reach his front door, but they kept blocking me, telling me that he was dead. And then when I finally reached the door, this woman with the face of an angel opened his door and invited me in. I pointed to the other women, standing all around the house and said, 'They told me Ronny was dead'. The woman laughed as she informed me that Ronny was indeed dead to those women, yet very much alive.

"I was confused at first, but I stepped into the house and there was Ronny, standing in a tub with a white rob on, drenched from head to toe as if he'd just been baptized."

Ramsey's face relaxed. He turned the light back out and lay back down.

"Are you going back to sleep, Ramsey? Don't you want to pray with me about this?"

"Yeah, I'm going back to sleep. I think God has already answered your prayers concerning Ronny. And once you digest the meaning of that dream, you'll go back to sleep, too."

Carmella wanted to turn the light back on, shake her husband, and do something, anything to make him stay up so they could pray together. But then her mind drifted back to her dream and little by little the meaning became clear. "Oh," she said as she lay back down and drifted off to a peaceful sleep.

Chapter 1

Ronny Thomas made more deals by 8:00 a.m. than most men made in a week. He was machine like when it came to wheeling, dealing and making his money. He'd always been like that, but just seven years ago he didn't even have enough money to pay his rent. Matter of fact, he didn't have any rent to pay because his older brothers, Ram and Dontae had allowed him to sleep on their couch while he rebuilt his life after yet another financial disaster had occurred. Back then Ronny dealt with a financial disaster just about every other week. But he'd known that if he ever got his hands on enough money to do business with, he would make something happen. And so he did.

After taking out a fifty thousand dollar loan, he was back in business. Forbes magazine now called him an overnight success, an internet and real estate mogul because of the two businesses he had finally mastered. It seemed everyone was singing his praises these days, but Ronny knew that none of it would have been possible if his brother, Ram wasn't the vice president of the bank that loaned him the money. Like they say... it's not what you know, but who you know. Ronny was convinced that there were so many men and women in the world who, if given a break like he had received, would be able to make a success out of their lives as well. So today, he was paying it forward. Ram was now the president of a local bank in Charlotte. Ronny had decided to partner with Ram's bank for the entrepreneurial program he wanted to get started. That way, it was like a double paying it forward... helping his brother's new bank and helping future entrepreneurs.

"They're ready for you, Mr. Thomas," a woman peeked her head into the room and told him.

Ronny smiled as he rose out of his seat. These days he was respected and called Mister everywhere he went. He liked the sound of respect, because he couldn't seem to get any of that during the years he struggled to find his way in the business world.

But he wasn't struggling anymore. Today, he was wearing a Valentino. The suit was Navy blue with a single-breasted jacket that had notched lapels and a two button center front fastening and matching pants with a slim straight leg. To dress the suit down a bit, Ronny chose a black roll neck sweater. But dressed down or not, he still looked like a million bucks. Ronny was living the dream; now... time to go make someone else's dreams come true.

***

Slicing the green apple and tossing it into a sandwich bag, Nia Brooks shouted, "Two minutes, Jarod." She could not afford to be late today. Everything was riding on her ability to get to the convention center and impress the formidable Mr. Ronald Thomas with her business plan.

"I'm on a pirate adventure, Mommy," Jarod, her adorable four-year-old son yelled from his room.

"Not this morning you're not. I have to get to an important meeting." Nia put his lunch box into her oversized purse and stomped off to her son's room. She opened the door and spotted him inside of the box that his Christmas present had come in.

"Will your boss be mad if you're late for your meeting?" Jarod asked with his pirate hat firmly secured to his head as he rowed his cardboard box of a ship with two thick sticks he'd found in the front yard of their apartment building.

Nia lamented over the sixty dollars she had splurged to spend on Christmas presents that were being ignored. If she'd gotten him a box and a few sticks, maybe she'd have the rest of the rent money needed to keep a roof over their heads this month. "The meeting I have isn't for work. It's with some very important people who could help Mommy get her new business up and running."

"If you're not going to work, then help me find the hidden treasure."

"I'm serious, Jarod. No more fooling around. This meeting is really important to Mommy."

"All right, all right." Jarod reluctantly climbed out of the box and put his coat on. As they were walking out the door, Jarod asked, "Can you go on a pirate adventure with me tonight?"

Nia handed her son his lunch box. As she was locking their apartment up, she nodded. "Sure thing, Captain. I'll be the first mate on the ship." After locking the door, she saluted him and then turned to leave the building. But a big imposing figure was blocking her way.

"Good morning, Mrs. Brooks, I was hoping to catch you before you left for work this morning."

"She's not going to work," Jarod provided unsolicited information.

"I have a meeting," Nia responded.

"I won't keep you. I just stopped by to fix the faucet in your bathroom and to collect the rent."

"About that..." Nia began.

Drake lifted a hand. "Before you say that you don't have it, I have to tell you that I'm in a bind. The owner of the building will be coming here to tour the complex tonight. He will be looking at the books. And there's no way that I can explain the fact that you've only been paying half the amount of your rent for the past two months."

"Can't you give me a little more time, Drake? Things have just been really hard lately, but you know I'll catch up on the rent."

He shook his head.

"A couple more days?" Nia hoped that the sad look in her eyes would cause Drake to help her out one more time. Since Johnny died she'd needed a lot of just-one-more-time kind of help. Nia never realized that making a living would be so hard. But after losing

Johnny's income and then being laid off from two jobs and then working temp jobs whenever she could get an assignment, reality hit her upside the head real quick.

She and Johnny had been so young when they married that life insurance had been the furthest thing from their minds. In Nia's wildest imagination, she never would have thought that Johnny would die of a heart attack the same day their son was born. Everything had been a struggle after that, and Nia had put her dreams of owning her own business on the back burner. Because the thing she most concerned herself with these days was keeping a roof over her and Jarod's heads.

"I can give you until two o'clock today, but that's it."

"Thanks, Drake." Nia walked away from him with a smile on her face, but what Drake couldn't see was that she was silently praying, asking God to fix this situation. She had twenty-five dollars to her name. But she'd used twelve dollars of that money in order to put a few professional touches to her business plan. She needed to put ten dollars in the gas tank, and Jarod needed two dollars for the field trip at his daycare.

"God, You know my needs... make a way out of no way," she kept saying within her spirit as she and Jarod drove down the street. It seemed as if her life had been about losing, because Nia didn't have much of anything. She'd lost her mother and father by the time she was twenty, her husband was gone before her twenty-fifth birthday. Several jobs had come and gone.

So, it was true that Nia had lost a lot, but she hadn't lost her faith. As far as Nia was concerned, her problems might be big, but her God was bigger.

Jarod's daycare was only two blocks away. They got out of the car. Nia held on to her son's hand as she escorted him into the center. She was so grateful that she had found this place, the weekly fee was reasonable, Jarod loved his teacher and was learning to read because of their phonics reading program.

"Are you excited to see Ms. Johnson?" Nia asked Jarod. He'd been in daycare the last three years and had always seemed so shy and withdrawn at the other daycare centers Nia had taken him to. But all that changed when he joined Ms. Johnson's class.

"Yea, I'm going to class. We're going on a field trip today."

She wished it had been a free field trip, but Nia wasn't going to be the one to ruin his fun. Especially since precious little of that was coming their way these days.

"Mrs. Brooks, can I speak with you for a moment?"

Nia was beginning to think that the only way she would get a break today would be if she fell down and broke her leg. Smiling like she'd done with Drake, Nia said, "Of course, Amanda. Just let me drop Jarod off to his class and I'll meet you in your office."

"I need to see you before you drop Jarod off."

Like she was marching to the guillotine, Nia turned and headed into Amanda's office with Jarod close by her side.

Amanda closed the door behind them, and without even offering them a seat she said, "We need to clear up your bill before Jarod can go to class today."

"What do you mean? I paid you last week."

With an empathy-filled expression, Amanda said, "I'm sorry, Nia but the check bounced. That's the second time since Jarod has been here, so my boss has instructed me to only take a money order from you from now on."

She hadn't realized that any of her checks had bounced. She'd paid the electric bill, paid on that stupid credit card that she no longer had access to, but still owed five thousand dollars on, bought groceries... oh that's right, she thought as her mind kept rewinding, she had a flat tire last week. She'd forgotten about the check that went to the auto club. "What can I say, Amanda? I didn't mean to write a bad check. The money was in my account when I wrote the check. But I had a flat tire, and I guess I just forgot about the checks I had already sent out."

"Believe me, Nia, I understand. I barely make enough here to keep the lights on in my apartment. But my boss is really upset about this second bad check."

Nia hated the situation she was in. As a Christian, she believed in paying her bills and having a good name. But lately her name was being run through the mud with everybody. Something was going to have to give. "I really need your help, Amanda. I don't have anywhere else I can take Jarod today. I have a meeting this morning that I can't miss. I promise that if you let him stay, I'll get the money that I owe in here within the next few days."

Amanda hesitated for a moment, but then said, "Well, I'm just going to get to the paperwork that's stacking up on my desk, I guess you must have slipped by me this morning."

Getting the meaning in her words, Nia hugged the woman. "Thank you so much, Amanda." She then rushed Jarod to his class. When she got back to her car and looked at the time, she realized that she had just twenty minutes to get uptown. With the way the morning traffic was in Charlotte, it was going to take her at least twenty five. She glanced over at her business plan and then looked toward heaven and said, "Lord, I need a miracle. Can you please rush me through traffic without allowing me to get a ticket that I cannot pay? Thank You, Jesus, send Your angels and let's be on our way."

You've been reading an excerpt of...

His Love Walk (Book 7)
Praise Him Anyhow Series

Excerpt of Book 1

Tears Fall at Night

by

Vanessa Miller

One

"I'm leaving you," Judge Nelson Marshall said, as he walked into the kitchen and stood next to the stainless steel prep table.

Taking a sweet potato soufflé out of her brand new Viking, dual-baking oven, Carmella was bobbing her head to Yolanda Adams's, "I Got the Victory", so she didn't hear Nelson walk into the kitchen.

He turned the music down and said, "Did you hear me, Carmella? I'm leaving."

Carmella put the soufflé on her prep table and turned toward Nelson. He was frowning, and she'd never known him to frown when she baked his favorite soufflé. Then she saw the suitcase in his hand and understood. Nelson hated to travel. His idea of the perfect vacation was staying home and renting movies for an entire week, but recently he had been attending one convention after another. And last week, he'd been in Chicago with her as she had to attend her brother's funeral.

Carmella was thankful that Nelson had taken vacation to attend the funeral with her, because she really didn't think she would have made it through that week without him. She and her younger brother had always been close, but after losing both their parents by the time they were in their thirties, the bond between them had become even stronger. Now she was trying to make sense of a world where forty-six-year-old men died of heart attacks.

Nelson had been fidgety the entire time they were in Chicago. She knew he hated being away from home, so she cut their trip short by a day. He hadn't told her he had another trip planned. "Not another one of those boring political conventions?"

He shook his head.

Nelson had almost lost his last bid for criminal court judge. Since then he had been obsessed with networking with government officials in hopes of getting appointed to a federal bench and bypassing elections altogether.

"Sit down, Carmella, we need to talk."

Carmella sat down on one of the stools in front of the kitchen island.

Nelson sat down next to Carmella. He lowered his head.

"Nelson, what's wrong?"

He didn't respond. But he had the same look on his face that he'd had the night they'd received the call about his grandmother's death.

"Please say something, honey. You're scaring me," Carmella said.

He lifted his head and attempted to look into his wife's eyes, but quickly turned away as he said, "This doesn't work for me anymore."

Confused, Carmella asked, "What's not working?"

"This marriage, Carmella. It's not what I want anymore."

"I don't understand, Nelson." She turned away from him and looked around her expansive kitchen. It had been redesigned a couple of years ago to ensure that she had everything she needed to throw the most lavish dinner parties that Raleigh, NC had ever seen. Nelson had told her that if he were ever going to get an appointment to a federal bench, he would need to network and throw fundraising campaigns for the senators and congressmen of North Carolina.

So she'd exchanged her kitchen table for a prep table, and installed the walk-in cooler to keep her salads and desserts at just the right temperature for serving. The Viking stove with its six burners and dual oven—one side convection and the other with an infrared broiler—had been her most expensive purchase. But the oven had been worth it. The infrared broiler helped her food to taste like restaurant-quality broiled food, and the convection side of the oven did amazing things with her pastries. She'd turned her home into a showplace in order to impress the guests who attended their legendary dinner parties. She had done everything Nelson had asked her to do, so Carmella couldn't understand why she was now in her kitchen listening to her husband say that he didn't want this anymore. "We've been happy, right?"

Nelson shook his head. "I haven't been happy with our marriage for a long time now."

"Then why didn't you say something? We could have gone to counseling or talked with Pastor Mitchell."

Nelson stood up. "It's too late for that. I've already filed for a divorce. All you need to do is sign the papers when you receive them, and then we can both move on with our lives."

Tears welled in Carmella's eyes as she realized that while she had been living in this house and sleeping in the same bed with Nelson, he had been seeing a divorce lawyer behind her back. "What about the kids, Nelson? What am I supposed to tell them?"

"Our children are grown, Carmella. You can't hide behind them anymore."

"What's that supposed to mean?" Carmella stood up, anger flashing in her eyes. "Dontae is only seventeen years old. He's still in high school and needs both his parents to help him make his transition into adulthood."

"I'm not leaving Dontae. He can come live with me if he wants."

"Oh, so now you want to take my son away from me, too? What's gotten into you, Nelson? When did you become so cruel?"

"I'm not trying to take Dontae away from you. I just know that raising a son can be difficult for a woman to do alone. So, I'm offering to take him with me."

"That's generous of you," Carmella said snidely. Then a thought struck her, and she asked, "Are you seeing someone? Is that it? Is this some midlife crisis that you're going through?"

"This is not about anyone else, Carmella. It's about the fact that we just don't work anymore."

Tears were flowing down her honey-colored cheeks. "But I still love you. I don't want a divorce."

"I don't have time to argue with you. Just sign the papers and let's get this over with."

She put her hands on her small hips and did the sista-sista neck roll, as her bob-styled hair swished from one side to the other. "We haven't argued in years. I have just gone with the flow and done whatever you wanted me to do. But on the day my husband packs his bags and asks me for a divorce, I think we should at least argue about that, don't you?"

He pointed at her and sneered as if her very presence offended him. "See, this is exactly why I waited so long to tell you. I knew you were going to act irrational."

"Irrational! Are you kidding me?" Carmella wanted to pull her hair out. The man standing in front of her was not her husband. He must have fallen, bumped his head and lost his fool mind. "What are we going to tell Joy and Dontae? I mean...you're not giving me anything to go on. We've been married twenty-five years and all of a sudden you just want out?"

"Like I said before, Joy and Dontae will be fine." He picked up his suitcase again and said, "I'm done discussing this. I'll be back to get the rest of my clothes. You should receive the divorce papers in a day or two. Just sign them and put them on the kitchen table." He headed toward the front door.

Following behind him, Carmella began screaming, "I'm not signing any divorce papers, so don't waste your time sending them here. And when you get off of whatever drug you're on, you'll be grateful that I didn't sign."

After opening the front door, Nelson turned to face his wife. With anger in his eyes, he said, "You better sign those papers or you'll regret it." He then stepped out of the house and slammed the door.

Carmella opened the door and ran after her husband. "Why are you doing this, Nelson? How am I supposed to pay the house note or our other bills if you leave me like this?"

"Get back in the house. You're making a scene."

"You spring this divorce on me without a second thought about my feelings, but you have the nerve to worry about the neighbors overhearing us?" Carmella shook her head in disgust. "I knew you were selfish, Nelson. But I never thought you were heartless."

He opened his car door and got in. "You're not going to make me feel guilty about this, Carmella. It's over between us. I want a divorce."

As Nelson backed out of the driveway, Carmella put her hands on her hips and shouted, "Well, you're not getting one!"

She stood barefoot, hands on hips, as Nelson turned what had seemed like an ordinary day into something awful and hideous. He backed out of the driveway—and out of her life—if what he said was to be believed. Carmella had been caught off guard...taken by surprise by this whole thing. Nelson had always been a family-values, family-first kind of man. He loved his children, and she'd thought he loved her as well. The family had attended church together and loved the Lord. But in the last year, Nelson had found one reason after another for not attending Sunday services.

"Are you okay?"

Carmella had been in a daze, watching Nelson drive out of her life; so she hadn't noticed that Cynthia Drake, their elderly next-door neighbor was outside doing her weekly gardening. Carmella wiped the tears from her face and turned toward the older woman.

"Is there anything I can do?" Cynthia asked, as she took off her gardening gloves.

"W-what just happened?" Carmella asked with confusion in her eyes.

"Come on," Cynthia said. She grabbed hold of Carmella's arm. "Let me get you back in the house."

"Why is everybody so obsessed with this house? It's empty, nobody in it but me. What am I supposed to do here alone?"

Cynthia guided Carmella back into the house and sat her down on the couch. "I'm going to get you something to drink." She disappeared into the kitchen and came back with a glass of iced tea and a can of Sunkist orange soda. "I didn't know which one you might want."

Carmella reached for the soda. "The iced tea is Nelson's. I don't drink it."

Cynthia sat down next to Carmella. She put her hand on Carmella's shoulder. "Do you want to talk?"

"Talk about what?" Carmella opened the Sunkist and took a sip. "I don't even know what's going on. I mean... I thought we were happy. I had no idea that Nelson wanted a divorce, but evidently, he's been planning this for a while."

"You need to get a divorce lawyer," Cynthia said.

"I don't want a divorce. I don't know what has gotten into Nelson, but he'll be back."

"You and Nelson have been married a long time, so I hope you're right. It would be a shame for him to throw away his marriage after all these years."

Carmella put the Sunkist down, put her head in her hands and started crying. This was too much for her. Nelson was the father of her children. He was supposed to love her for the rest of her life. They had stood before God and vowed to be there for each other, through the good and the bad, until death. How could he do this to her?

"Here, hon. Dry your face." Cynthia handed Carmella some tissue. "Do you have any family members that I could call to have them come sit with you for a while?"

"My parents have been dead for years and my only brother died last week," she said miserably.

"Oh hon, I'm so sorry to hear that."

Carmella lifted her hands and then let them flap back into her lap. "I just don't understand. I thought we were happy."

Sitting down next to Carmella, Cynthia said, "I've been married three times, and honey, trust me when I tell you that you'll probably never understand. Men don't need a reason for the things they do."

They sat talking for a while, and Carmella was comforted by the wise old woman who had taken time out from her gardening to sit with her in her time of need. When Cynthia was ready to leave, Carmella felt as if she should do something for the kindly old woman. She ran to the kitchen and came back with the sweet potato soufflé that she had lovingly fixed for her husband. She handed it to Cynthia, and said, "Thank you. I don't know what I would have done if you hadn't helped me back into the house."

"Oh, sweetie, it was no problem. You don't have to give me anything."

"I want to. I made this sweet potato soufflé for my husband. But since he doesn't want it, it would bring me great joy knowing that another family enjoyed it."

"Well, then I'll take it."

After Carmella walked Cynthia out, she went to the upstairs bathroom. She lit her bathroom candles, turned on the hot water and then poured some peach scented bubble bath in the water. She got into the tub, hoping to soak her weary bones until the ache in her heart drifted away. The warm water normally soothed her and took her mind off the things that didn't get done that day or the things that didn't turn out just the way she'd planned. Carmella enjoyed the swept-away feeling she experienced when surrounded by bubbles and her vanilla-scented candles. But tonight, all she felt was dread. She wondered if anyone would care if she drifted off to sleep, slid down all the way into the water and drowned like Whitney Houston had done.

The thought was tempting, because Carmella didn't know if she wanted to live without her husband. Tears rolled down her face as she realized that as much as she didn't want to live without Nelson, he was already living without her.

You've been reading an excerpt of…

Tears Fall at Night (Book 1)
Praise Him Anyhow Series… the book that started the 9-book series

Other Books by Vanessa Miller

After the Rain
How Sweet The Sound
Heirs of Rebellion
Feels Like Heaven
Heaven on Earth
The Best of All
Better for Us
Her Good Thing
Long Time Coming
A Promise of Forever Love
A Love for Tomorrow
Yesterday's Promise
Forgotten
Forgiven
Forsaken
Rain for Christmas (Novella)
Through the Storm
Rain Storm
Latter Rain
Abundant Rain
Former Rain

Anthologies (Editor)
Keeping the Faith
Have A Little Faith
This Far by Faith

EBOOKS

Love Isn't Enough

A Mighty Love

The Blessed One (Blessed and Highly Favored series)

The Wild One (Blessed and Highly Favored Series)

The Preacher's Choice (Blessed and Highly Favored Series)

The Politician's Wife (Blessed and Highly Favored Series)

The Playboy's Redemption (Blessed and Highly Favored Series)

Tears Fall at Night (Praise Him Anyhow Series)

Joy Comes in the Morning (Praise Him Anyhow Series)

A Forever Kind of Love (Praise Him Anyhow Series)

Ramsey's Praise (Praise Him Anyhow Series)

Escape to Love (Praise Him Anyhow Series)

Praise For Christmas (Praise Him Anyhow Series)

His Love Walk (Praise Him Anyhow Series)

Could This Be Love (Praise Him Anyhow Series)

Song of Praise (Praise Him Anyhow Series)

About the Author

Vanessa Miller is a best-selling author, playwright, and motivational speaker. She started writing as a child, spending countless hours either reading or writing poetry, short stories, stage plays and novels. Vanessa's creative endeavors took on new meaning in1994 when she became a Christian. Since then, her writing has been centered on themes of redemption, often focusing on characters facing multi-dimensional struggles.

Vanessa's novels have received rave reviews, with several appearing on *Essence Magazine's* Bestseller's List. Miller's work has receiving numerous awards, including "Best Christian Fiction Mahogany Award" and the "Red Rose Award for Excellence in Christian Fiction." Miller graduated from Capital University with a degree in Organizational Communication. She is an ordained minister in her church, explaining, "God has called me to minister to readers and to help them rediscover their place with the Lord."

Vanessa has recently completed the For Your Love series for Kimani Romance and How Sweet the Sound for Abingdon Press, first book in a historical set in the Gospel era which releases March 2014. Vanessa is currently working on an ebook series of novellas in the Praise Him Anyhow series. She is also working on the My Soul to Keep series for Whitaker House.

Vanessa Miller's website address is: www.vanessamiller.com But you can also stay in touch with Vanessa by joining her mailing list @ http://vanessamiller.com/events/join-mailing-list/ Vanessa can also be reached at these other sites as well:

Join me on Facebook: https://www.facebook.com/groups/77899021863/

Join me on Twitter: https://www.twitter.com/vanessamiller01

Don't forget to join my mailing list:
http://vanessamiller.com/events/join-mailing-list/
Join me on Facebook: https://www.facebook.com/groups/77899021863/
Join me on Twitter: https://www.twitter.com/vanessamiller01

Next books in the series
His Love Walk (Rel. Feb. 2014)

Other Books in the Praise Him Anyhow series

Tears Fall at Night (Book 1 - Praise Him Anyhow Series)

Joy Comes in the Morning (Book 2 - Praise Him Anyhow Series)
A Forever Kind of Love (Book 3 - Praise Him Anyhow Series)

Ramsey's Praise (Book 4 - Praise Him Anyhow Series)

Escape to Love (Book 5 - Praise Him Anyhow Series)

Other Books by Vanessa Miller
The Best of All
Better for Us
Her Good Thing
Long Time Coming
A Promise of Forever Love
A Love for Tomorrow
Yesterday's Promise
Forgotten
Forgiven
Forsaken
Rain for Christmas (Novella)
Through the Storm
Rain Storm
Latter Rain
Abundant Rain
Former Rain
Anthologies (Editor)
Keeping the Faith
Have A Little Faith
This Far by Faith

EBOOKS

Love Isn't Enough

A Mighty Love

The Blessed One (Blessed and Highly Favored series)

The Wild One (Blessed and Highly Favored Series)

The Preacher's Choice (Blessed and Highly Favored Series)

The Politician's Wife (Blessed and Highly Favored Series)

The Playboy's Redemption (Blessed and Highly Favored Series)

Tears Fall at Night (Praise Him Anyhow Series)

Joy Comes in the Morning (Praise Him Anyhow Series)

A Forever Kind of Love (Praise Him Anyhow Series)

Ramsey's Praise (Praise Him Anyhow Series)

Escape to Love (Praise Him Anyhow Series)

Praise for Christmas (Praise Him Anyhow Series)

His Love Walk (Praise Him Anyhow Series)

Coming Feb. 2014

CPSIA information can be obtained
at www.ICGtesting.com
Printed in the USA
LVOW01s0908080516
487239LV00019B/483/P